THE ADVENTURES OF TOM SAWYER

by MARK TWAIN

#3 The Birthday Boy

Adapted by Catherine Nichols

Illustrated by Amy Bates

STERLING CHILDREN'S BOOKS

New York

STERLING CHILDREN'S BOOKS and the distinctive Sterling Children's Books logo are registered trademarks of Sterling Publishing Co., Inc.

Text © 2007 Sterling Publishing Co., Inc.
Illustrations © 2007 Amy Bates

ISBN 978-1-4027-4268-2

Distributed in Canada by Sterling Publishing Co., Inc.
c/o Canadian Manda Group, 664 Annette Street
Toronto, Ontario M6S 2C8, Canada
Distributed in the United Kingdom by GMC Distribution Services
Castle Place, 166 High Street, Lewes, East Sussex BN7 1XU, England
Distributed in Australia by NewSouth Books
University of New South Wales, Sydney, NSW 2052, Australia

Manufactured in the United States of America

Lot #:
10 9 8 7 6
07/20

sterlingpublishing.com

For information about custom editions, special sales, and premium and corporate purchases, please contact Sterling Special Sales at 800-805-5489 or specialsales@sterlingpublishing.com.

Contents

Tattletale

Tom Sawyer ran
all the way home.
He had been fishing.
What a fun day he'd had!
Tom saw his brother Sid
in the front yard.
Sid was raking leaves
into a big pile.
A frown was on his face.

"Where were you?" Sid asked.

"Fishing," said Tom.

"Aunt Polly told you to help
me," Sid said. "I had to do
all the chores myself."

Just then, Aunt Polly
came down the road.
Tom hid his fishing pole
behind a tree.
"Don't tell Aunt Polly
where I was," Tom said.

Aunt Polly opened the gate.
"I see all the leaves are raked,"
she said. "What a good job.
You boys may both
have some apple pie."

Sid mumbled something.
"What did you say, Sid?"
Aunt Polly asked.
"Only I should get pie,"
Sid told his aunt.
"I did all the work!"

"What?" Aunt Polly cried.

"Tom went fishing," said Sid.

"Look, Aunt Polly!"

Sid pointed to the fishing pole.

Aunt Polly picked up
the fishing pole.
"Is that true, Tom?"
asked Aunt Polly.
Tom nodded.
"I'm sorry," he said.

"Go to your room,"
said Aunt Polly.
"There will be no pie
for you, Tom."

Tom glared at Sid.
"Tattletale," Tom said.
"I'll get you for this!"
Tom stomped off
to his room.

Crash!

The next day
was Sid's birthday.
Sid was having a party.
He invited Tom.
Tom was still angry
with Sid, though.
So he decided
he would not go.

Then Tom saw Sid's
big birthday cake.
It was one of
Tom's favorites—
banana cream
with white frosting.

Tom's mouth watered.
He decided to go
to Sid's party after all.
Tom sat down at the table.

Aunt Polly brought in
bowls of blueberries.
She set a bowl
in front of each boy.
Then she went
to get the cream.

Tom sprinkled sugar
on his blueberries.
"Pass the sugar," Sid said.
Tom pushed the bowl
over to Sid.
Some sugar spilled.
"You spilled the sugar
on purpose!" Sid said.
"I did not!" said Tom.
"I'm telling Aunt Polly
on you," Sid said.

"Go ahead," said Tom,
"but pass the sugar
back over here first."
Sid gave the bowl
a hard push. . . .
Crash! It fell to the floor!

The Confession

Aunt Polly came back
with the cream.
She had seen
Sid push the bowl.
She had seen it
crash to the floor.
Her nephews did not
know she had seen it.

Tom was going to enjoy
seeing Sid get in trouble
for a change!
Then Tom saw Sid's face.
It was very pale, and Sid's
eyes were very wide.

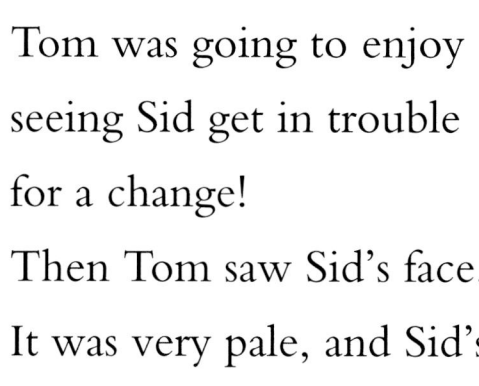

Tom suddenly felt bad
for his brother and said,
"Aunt Polly, I'm very sorry.
I broke the bowl."
"Tom, that is a lie,"
said Aunt Polly.

"I saw what happened.
Sid broke the bowl.
Now, both of you boys,
go upstairs to your room."
"What did I do?" Tom asked.
"Think about it," said Aunt Polly.

The Birthday Wish

Tom sat on his bed.
Sid sat across from him.
They were very quiet.
Tom tried to figure out
what he had done.
All he could think about
was the cake downstairs.

The two brothers sat silently.
After a while, Sid said,
"Tom, I broke the bowl.
Why did you take the blame?"
"I have more practice
getting in trouble than you,"
said Tom. "I'm better at it."

"Aunt Polly says it's
not nice to lie," said Sid,
"but it was nice of you to try
to keep me out of trouble."
Tom blushed. "I guess," he said.

They sat quietly again
until Aunt Polly walked in.
"If you boys have learned
your lesson," she said,
"you may come eat cake."

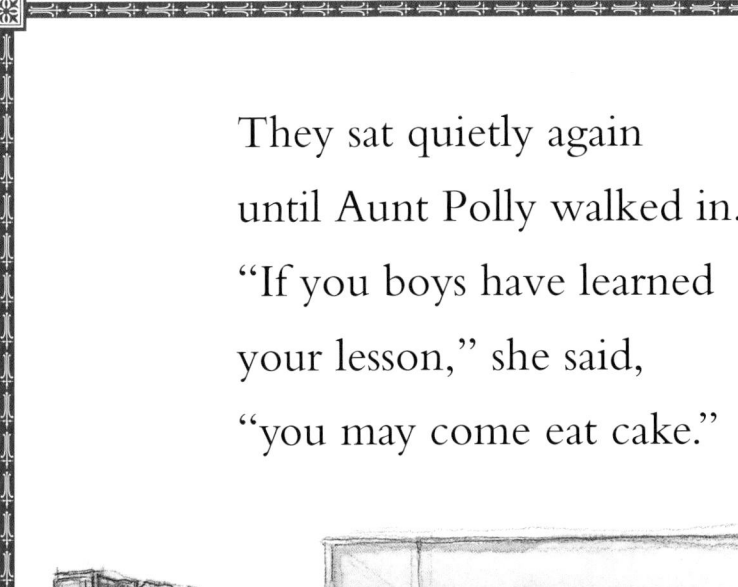

Suddenly, Tom figured out
why his aunt had sent him
to his room along with Sid.
"I have learned my lesson!"
Tom said. "I was just telling Sid
that it's not nice to lie."

"That is a lie!" said Sid.

"I was telling that to Tom!"

Aunt Polly threw up her hands.

"No cake for you, Tom!" she said.

"Only Sid may come with me."

Sid started to follow his aunt.

Then he saw Tom's face.
It was very sad, and Tom's
eyes were filled with tears.
Sid suddenly felt bad
for his brother.

"Aunt Polly, I would like to make
my birthday wish now, before
I blow out the candles," Sid said.
"I wish Tom could come eat cake."
"All right," said Aunt Polly,
"if that is what you wish, Sid."

"Sid, that was nice!" said Tom,
as they all went downstairs.
Sid blushed. "I guess," he said.
"On my birthday," said Tom,
"I was going to wish for
a whole cake just for me.
Now I'm going to wish for two—
one for me and one for you!"
Sid smiled at his brother.
"That sounds fine, Tom," Sid said.
"That sounds just fine."